DEC 2007

Ivan

the Terrier

by Peter Catalanotto

A Richard Jackson Book · Atheneum Books for Young Readers · New York London Toronto Sydney

Atheneum Books for Young Readers

An imprint of Simon & Schuster Children's Publishing Division

1230 Avenue of the Americas, New York, New York 10020

Book design by Ann Bobco

The text for this book is set in Fairplex.

The illustrations for this book are rendered in watercolor and gouache.

Manufactured in Mexico

First Edition

10 9 8 7 6 5 4 3 2

Library of Congress Cataloging-in-Publication Data

Catalanotto, Peter.

Ivan the terrier / Peter Catalanotto.—1st ed.

p. cm.

"A Richard Jackson Book."

 Summary: A terrier named Ivan keeps interrupting story hour.

ISBN-13: 978-1-4169-1247-7

ISBN-10: 1-4169-1247-9

1. Terriers—Juvenile fiction. [1. Terriers—Fiction. 2. Dogs—Fiction. 3. Books and reading—Fiction. 4. Storytelling—Fiction.] I. Title.

PZ10.3.C29346Iva 2007

[E]—dc22

2006010812

To My Baby Bear

Once upon a time there were
three billy goats named Gruff.

Hey, where did that dog come from?

Is that Ivan?

It is!

Arf! Arf! Arf!
Arf!
Arf! Arf!
Arf!
Arf! Arf!

Ivan!
You naughty dog!
You're ruining the story!

Ivan! Get back here!

Ivan!

Oh well.

I guess we'll have to read
a different story.

Once upon a time,
deep in the forest,
there lived three bears.

Oh, **no!**
Sit! Ivan! **Sit!**

Arf!

Arf! Arf!
Arf!
Arf! Arf! Arf!
Arf!
Arf!

This story
is **not**
about you!

Bad dog!

Heel!

Ivan!
Heel!

Oh dear. Let's try another one.

Once upon a time there were
three little pigs . . .

Ivan!

Ivan, stop!

You come back here right now!

Ivan!

My word. I've never seen anything like this.

Once upon a time a little old lady baked a gingerbread boy for her husband because the two of them were lonely.

Oh, come **on!**
Would somebody please grab that dog?

Ivan! Sit!

Ivan!
Drop it!

Shame on you!

Don't eat that!

Ugh.

All right. I give up.

There once was
a little dog named Ivan.

Now where is he going?

Oh.
I see.

Good night, Ivan.